✔ KU-311-569

ROB CHILDS

COUNTY CUP

Book Three
The South Quarter

Cup Shocks

Illustrated by Robin Lawrie

Cavan County Library
Withdrawn Stock

CORGI YEARLING BOOKS

CAVAN COUNTY LIBRARY
ACC No. C103212
CLASS NO. J
INVOICE NO 4562 Laburnum
PRICE £2.00

CUP SHOCKS
A CORGI YEARLING BOOK : 0 440 863856

First publication in Great Britain

PRINTING HISTORY
Corgi Yearling edition published 2000

1 3 5 7 9 10 8 6 4 2

Copyright © 2000 by Rob Childs
Illustrations copyright © 2000 by Robin Lawrie

Cover photograph shot on location at Northolt High School
by Oliver Hunter

With thanks to the staff and pupils of Northolt High School for their
help in the preparation of the cover.

The right of Rob Childs to be identified as the author of this work
has been asserted in accordance with the Copyright, Designs
and Patents Act 1988

Condition of Sale
This book is sold subject to the condition that it shall not, by way of
trade or otherwise, be lent, re-sold, hired out or otherwise circulated
without the publisher's prior consent in any form of binding or
cover other than that in which it is published and without a
similar condition including this condition being imposed on the
subsequent purchaser.

Set in 12/15 pt New Century Schoolbook by
Phoenix Typesetting, Ilkley, West Yorkshire

Corgi Yearling Books are published by Transworld Publishers,
61–63 Uxbridge Road, Ealing, London W5 5SA,
a division of The Random House Group Ltd,
in Australia by Random House Australia (Pty) Ltd,
20 Alfred Street, Milsons Point, Sydney, NSW 2061, Australia,
in New Zealand by Random House New Zealand Ltd,
18 Poland Road, Glenfield, Auckland 10, New Zealand
and in South Africa by Random House (Pty) Ltd,
Endulini, 5a Jubilee Road, Parktown 2193, South Africa.

Made and printed in Great Britain by
Cox & Wyman Ltd, Reading, Berkshire

Class No. _____J_____ Acc No. C103212

Author: Childs, R   Loc: 7 - MAY 2001

LEABHARLANN
CHONDAE AN CHABHAIN

- 9 AUG 2002

1. This book may be kept three weeks. It is to be returned on / before the last date stamped below.
2. A fine of 20p will be charged for every week or part of week a book is overdue.

5 OCT 2001		
9 MAR 2002		
2 8 MAY 2004		
1 OCT 2004		
2 9 JAN 2005		
- 2 MAR 2005		
2 0 APR 2005		

Also available by Rob Childs,
and published by Corgi Yearling Books:

County Cup Series
1: CUP FAVOURITES
2: CUP RIVALS
3. CUP SHOCKS
4: CUP CLASHES

Coming soon:
5: CUP GLORY
6: CUP FEVER
7: CUP WINNERS

Soccer Mad series
FOOTBALL FANATIC   SOCCER MAD
ALL GOALIES ARE CRAZY   FOOTBALL DAFT
FOOTBALL FLUKES   SOCCER STARS

SOCCER MAD COLLECTION
includes SOCCER MAD, ALL GOALIES ARE CRAZY

SOCCER AT SANDFORD
SANDFORD ON TOUR

Published by Young Corgi Books:

The Big series
THE BIG GAME   THE BIG WIN
THE BIG MATCH   THE BIG PRIZE
THE BIG DAY   THE BIG KICK
THE BIG GOAL   THE BIG CLASH
THE BIG BREAK   THE BIG CHANCE
THE BIG STAR   THE BIG FREEZE
THE BIG FIX   THE BIG DROP

THE BIG FOOTBALL COLLECTION
includes THE BIG GAME, THE BIG MATCH, THE BIG PRIZE

THE BIG FOOTBALL FEAST
includes THE BIG DAY, THE BIG KICK, THE BIG GOAL

THE BIG FOOTBALL TREBLE
includes THE BIG BREAK, THE BIG CHANCE, THE BIG STAR

Published by Corgi Pups,
for beginner readers:

GREAT SAVE!
GREAT SHOT!

INTRODUCTION

Long ago, the historic county of Medland was made up of four separate regions. These divisions can now only be found on ancient maps, but people living in the old North, South, East and West Quarters still remain loyal to their own area.

One way that the traditional rivalry between the Quarters is kept up is by means of the County Cup.

Every year, schools from all over the county take part in this great soccer tournament and the standard of football is always high. Matches are played on a local group basis at first to decide the Quarter Champions, who will then clash in the knockout stages of the competition later in the season.

The winners receive the much-prized silver trophy and earn the right to call themselves the County Champions – the top team in Medland.

THE COUNTY OF MEDLAND

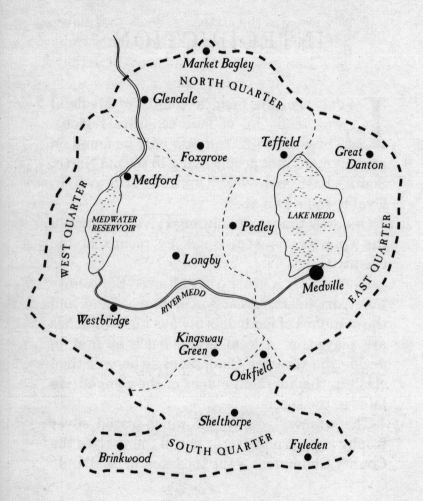

Market Bagley

NORTH QUARTER

Glendale

Teffield

Great Danton

Foxgrove

WEST QUARTER

Medford

MEDWATER RESERVOIR

LAKE MEDD

Pedley

Longby

Medville

EAST QUARTER

RIVER MEDD

Westbridge

Kingsway Green

Oakfield

Shelthorpe

Fyleden

SOUTH QUARTER

Brinkwood

SCHOOLS

FOXGROVE

GLENDALE

GREAT
DANTON

LAKEVIEW

FYLEDEN

OAKFIELD

HILLCREST

KINGSWAY
GREEN

MARKET
BAGLEY

TEFFIELD

MEDVILLE

SIR GEORGE
NEEDHAM

SHELTHORPE

ST WYSTAN'S

RIVERSIDE

WESTBRIDGE

These are the sixteen schools that have qualified to play in the County Cup this season – try and see where they are on the map . . .

NORTH QUARTER

Foxgrove High School
Glendale Community School
Market Bagley Community School
Teffield Comprehensive School

EAST QUARTER

Great Danton High School
Lakeview High School, Medville
Medville Comprehensive School
Sir George Needham Community College,
Pedley

SOUTH QUARTER

Fyleden Community College
Oakfield High School
Shelthorpe Comprehensive School
St Wystan's Comprehensive School,
Brinkwood

WEST QUARTER

Hillcrest Comprehensive School, Longby
Kingsway Green High School
Riverside Comprehensive School, Medford
Westbridge Community College

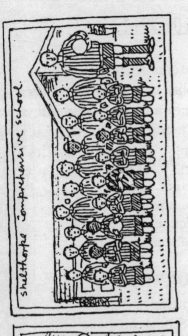

Shelthorpe Comprehensive school

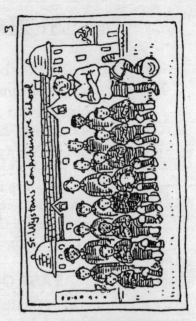

St Wystan's Comprehensive school

Tyledon Community College

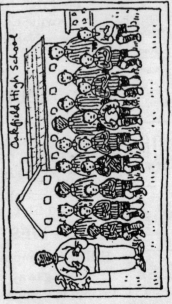

Oakfield High School

MEET THE TEAMS

The autumn term is a month old: soccer trials have been held, squads selected, a few league and friendly matches already played – and now it's time for the County Cup. Four schools in the South Quarter of Medland have qualified to take part in this season's competition, including the Cup holders.

The opening fixtures in the round-robin group are:

St Wystan's Comprehensive School v Shelthorpe Comprehensive School

Oakfield High School v Fyleden Community College

Meet the teams on the next few pages and perhaps even choose one that you might like to support in their games. Then follow their fortunes in this book to see what happens in the exciting quest for the County Cup.

Who will be Champions of the South?

Read on and find out . . .

FYLEDEN COMMUNITY COLLEGE

Small secondary school in the market town of Fyleden near the southern boundary of Medland.

Headteacher: *Mr David Senior*
Head of P.E. Dept: *Mr Ken Tyler*
School colours: *yellow shirts, blue shorts, yellow socks*
Year 7 soccer captain: *Stuart Kaye*
Usual team formation: *4–3–3*

Year 7 soccer squad:

Simon Osborne (Oz)

Pat O'Brien   Dan Bentley   Stuart Kaye   Gary Noble

Vijay Chauhan   Ronnie Todd   Joe Healey

Jeff Crooke (Bandit)   Neil Lewis   Colin McCann

plus:
Chris Banks, Sean Mills, Darryl Silver, Diviesh Poonia, Graham Watts, Adam Kenning

10

CAPTAIN'S *Notes...*

We don't care if some people reckon we're the group's underdogs. At a recent area team trial, kids from the other schools said they'd thrash us just because Shelthorpe beat us 5—0 in a friendly. So what? Wait till the real thing starts and we'll show 'em we can play a bit.

Our rivals might have better squads on paper but like Mr Tyler says, it's what happens on the pitch that matters. The main reason we lost that game was that Oz, our first-choice keeper, is out of action for a while with an injured wrist. Ronnie, the team joker, told winger Jeff Crooke (nicknamed Bandit) that he ought to put his arm in a sling as well — just so we could then call him a one-armed Bandit!

Anyway, you'll be able to judge us for yourselves soon. Watch out for Vijay's tricky dribbling, Bandit's speed, Ronnie's rocket shots, big Neil's heading and — hopefully — Oz's brilliant goalkeeping. We'll be OK, don't worry — and we might even surprise a few people along the way.

OAKFIELD HIGH SCHOOL

Medium-sized secondary school in the village of Oakfield, situated in the northern tip of the South Quarter. Pupils in year groups 7, 8 and 9 only, aged between 11 and 14.

Headteacher: *Mrs Sally Unwin*
P.E. teacher: *Mr Maurice Bradley*
School colours: *black and white striped shirts, black shorts and socks*
Year 7 soccer captain: *Ross Collins*
Usual team formation: *4–1–3–2 (sweeper system)*

Year 7 soccer squad:

Andrew White

Parminder Singh   Suresh Chand   Hugh Morris   Dean Porter

Ross Collins

Tom Neville (Nev) Paul Ward   Nathan Grant

Martin Hudson   Sunjit Gill (Sunny)

plus:
Iqbal Sayeed, Carl Burgess, Tim Larwood, Phil Kelly, Sam Dixon, Lawrence Ilott (Lorry), Ben Temple

12

We're a red-hot attacking team so don't come to our games expecting to watch boring 0—0 draws. It'll be all-out attack, I promise. Our teacher says he's not worried about how many goals we let in so long as we score even more at the other end. That's fine by us. Goals are what football's all about.

We've got two brilliant strikers, Martin Hudson and Sunny Gill. Martin's real class. I reckon he might even make it big-time as a star pro one day. As for me, I play as a kind of sweeper in front of the defence, always looking for the chance to break forward and join in our attacks. Dean and Parminder will be overlapping up the wings as well whenever they can and all the midfield players can score goals. We got tons of them for our village primary school in the last couple of seasons.

It's sure to be exciting stuff. We want to try and set a new County Cup goal-scoring record!

SHELTHORPE COMPREHENSIVE

Large comprehensive school in the town of Shelthorpe in the centre of the South Quarter.

Headteacher: *Mr Sebastian Smith*
Head of P.E. Dept: *Mr Ronald Calvert*
School colours: *blue and white striped shirts, blue shorts and socks*
Year 7 soccer captain: *Matthew Eales*
Usual team formation: *4–2–4*

Year 7 soccer squad:

Tom Humphreys

(Gladys)
Harry Gladwin   Robin Cheetham   Liam Walsh   Scott Hinton

Matthew Eales   Jack Naylor

Kevin Ashby   Ian Strong   Sadiq Jilani   Jonathan Shaw

plus:
Paul Jones, Charnjit Rai, Andy Robinson, Farid Ali, George Osman, James Butcher, Alun Morgan

CAPTAIN'S
Notes...

We've got a lot to live up to this season. Last year's Comp team actually went and won the County Cup! Shelthorpe were the first school from the South Quarter to win the competition for fifteen years. As holders, there's nothing we'd love more than to go right through to the Final again and retain the trophy. That'd make me dead proud as captain. And I'm determined to make that dream come true.

I play in midfield with Jack mostly, although we might sometimes switch from a 4–2–4 formation to 4–3–3 or 4–4–2. Ian and Sadiq will probably be our chief goalscorers, but there's quite a few guys who'll be expecting to get their names on the scoresheet regularly – including me.

Our defence has looked pretty solid in the first two league games – both won easily – so there's no reason why we can't keep the Cup in Shelthorpe's packed trophy cabinet next to the Quarter Shield. Stick with us if you want to be on the winning side.

ST WYSTAN'S COMPREHENSIVE SCHOOL

Medium-sized comprehensive school in the village of Brinkwood on the west side of the South Quarter.

Headteacher: *Mr Roy Daniels*
P.E. teacher: *Mr Larry Cooper*
School colours: *all-green*
Year 7 football captain: *Simon James*
Usual team formation: *4–3–3*

Year 7 football squad:

Mark Brown

Josh Rowlands   Graham Nixon   Steve Varley   Ben Udal

Stuart O'Leary   Lee Melling   Michael Earl

Jagdish Hira (Jag)   David Butler   Simon James

plus:
Kushal Bhatia, Pete Chambers, Ryan Witchell, Keith Stewart, Eddie Kirk

16

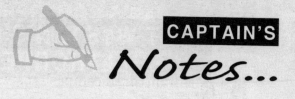

CAPTAIN'S
Notes...

As captain of the Saints' Year 7 soccer squad, it's a good job I enjoy writing. Besides scribbling a few lines here, I've been asked by the editor of the school's student magazine to write a regular diary piece about what happens to us in the County Cup. I'm going to call it Captain's Log! Blame my dad for the corny title, but I'm really looking forward to doing the reports after each of our games.

The midfield is probably the strongest area of our team with Lee, Stuart and Mike, but the defence looks good enough not to let in too many goals. Up front, me and Jag on the wings will be trying to supply the ammunition for the likes of Dave or Eddie to fire home.

What are the Saints' chances in the Cup? Well, now that Shelthorpe have finally broken the South Quarter jinx, perhaps it will be our turn to win it this season. That might be wishful thinking, but we'll soon find out how good we are. Our first match is against Shelthorpe. It could be a very short-term diary!

ST WYSTAN'S v SHELTHORPE

Saturday 4 October
k.o. 9.45 a.m.
Referee: Mr L. Cooper

. . . let's start on the Cup trail by seeing how the holders begin their defence of the trophy at St Wystan's – the teams are just lining up with Shelthorpe in the stripes attacking the goal to our left . . .

Matthew Eales ran up to eyeball each of his Shelthorpe side in turn, demanding one hundred per cent effort and concentration.

'Keep your mind on the game, Tom,' he told his goalie, catching him glancing at a girl by the corner flag.

'Nobody beats you in the air today, Liam, right . . . ?'

'C'mon, Gladys, wakey-wakey, you look half asleep . . .'

'We want a goal from you this morning, Sadiq, OK?'

Shelthorpe's coach, Mr Calvert, nodded in satisfaction as he watched Matt's pre-match routine from the touchline. The boy's forceful personality was the main reason he'd been made captain.

'I might as well go home and leave it up to Matt now,' he remarked to a colleague who had helped with transport. 'He's doing my job for me.'

'A bit different to his older brother, eh?'

'You're not kidding. Nothing but trouble, that Jason. Thank goodness he's left now. I was glad to see the back of him.'

'We all were. I groaned when I saw we had another Eales coming up from the primary school this year, but they're chalk and cheese.'

To no-one's great surprise it was the captain who made the first important tackle of the game. Matt broke up a raid on the edge of his own penalty area and then swept the ball out to the wing to start a counter-attack.

'Take the man on, Kev, lick him,' he shouted.

Kevin Ashby pushed the ball past his marker and sprinted hard, but the defender was no slouch. He matched the winger for speed and finally slid the ball out of play for a throw-in. It was an early indication that the Cup holders were not going to have everything their own way.

Indeed, if anything, the home side had the better of the opening quarter of an hour, despite Matt's continued cajoling of his players. His opposing captain, Simon James, was on good form on the Saints' left wing. The visitors' vulnerable number two often needed extra help to stop the winger dribbling his way through or curling dangerous crosses into the goalmouth.

'Get tighter on him, Gladys,' Matt barked. 'Don't give him so much space to run at you.'

'I'm trying, I'm trying,' the full-back panted. 'It's not easy, y'know, he keeps dropping so deep.'

'Well, go with him. You'll have to man-mark him. I'll cover behind you.'

The next time Simon picked up the ball in his own half, he found Gladys snapping at his heels straight away. The winger shielded the ball long enough to allow a teammate to come up in support and then played a neat one-two to escape Gladys's shackles. Simon strode over the halfway line in possession, leaving Gladys stumbling in his wake, and lofted the ball into the middle before Matt could put in a challenge.

Centre-back Liam won the aerial duel for the ball, but it ran loose to another striker who hit a fierce drive on target. Only a smart save from Tom prevented Shelthorpe from going a goal down.

Mr Calvert decided to act without delay to strengthen the midfield. His team was being outnumbered and outplayed in that crucial area of the pitch. 'Sub, ref, please,' he called, waving his arms to attract the attention of the referee, who blew his whistle to hold up play. 'Switch to 4–3–3, lads. Get them organized, Matt.'

The captain told the substitute to cover Gladys, leaving himself freer to try and take control of midfield. But it was in this period of transition that the Saints scored a well-deserved goal. For a change, the threat came from the right wing. With Tom anticipating a centre, the unexpected low shot fooled the keeper and sneaked inside the near post.

'This is rubbish!' Matt fumed as the Saints celebrated their success. 'We're supposed to be the County Champions – so let's start playing like it.'

His teammates responded, twice forcing the Saints goalie into serious action, but they were still trailing 1–0 at the interval. They braced themselves for another bout of tongue-lashing, this time from a grim-faced Mr Calvert.

The second half told a different story. A galvanized Shelthorpe clearly meant business. They worked so hard, it seemed almost as if they had two extra players on the field. They certainly had two defenders sticking very close to Simon to mark him out of the game. Gladys wasn't one of them. He'd been replaced by another substitute.

The Saints were no longer allowed to settle on the ball. They found themselves hustled and harassed, bustled and badgered in all parts of the pitch. Every time a green-shirted player received the ball, two or three blue and white striped ones immediately closed him down.

Matthew Eales was the inspiration. The captain led by example, chasing, blocking, tackling, shouting – and finally scoring. His rising shot clipped the underside of the bar and buried itself in the bottom of the netting like an unexploded bomb.

The Saints keeper had no chance either with the second goal just three minutes later. He was left helpless by Kevin's pinpoint centre that floated over everybody's head until landing perfectly on Sadiq's black curls at the far post. The striker couldn't miss from only two metres out.

The Saints failed to recover from that double whammy, with Matt refusing to let anybody relax until the final whistle. Tom barely had a touch in the second period – and the same went for Simon too.

'We thought we had you beat there at half-time,' he said ruefully as the two captains shook hands afterwards.

'No way!' Matt grinned, delighted with his side's spirited comeback. 'Somebody's gonna have to play dead well – *all* game – to tear our hands off that Cup.'

'Oh well, there's nothing we can do now to loosen your grip,' Simon sighed. 'This was our big chance and we've blown it.'

Result:	St Wystan's	1 v 2	Shelthorpe
		h-t: 1 – 0	
Scorers:	Hira		Eales
			Jilani

OAKFIELD v FYLEDEN

Saturday 4 October
k.o. 10 a.m.
Referee: Mr M. Bradley

. . . Phew! Just got time to catch the last few minutes of the other opening game if we hurry – Oakfield's top striker Martin Hudson has already celebrated his twelfth birthday with a hat-trick and he's still looking for more presents . . .

'**C**'mon, ref, blow that whistle,' muttered Fyleden's teacher, glancing again at his watch. 'Put us out of our misery.'

Mr Tyler had spent a wretched morning watching his weakened team torn apart by the home side's fast-flowing football. Beset by injury and illness, they'd been able to offer little resistance and were 4–1 down. Even Stuart Kaye, their captain and centre-back, had found Oakfield's powerful attack too much of a handful

– especially the tall number nine. He looked a class apart.

Oakfield won their umpteenth corner of the match and the ball was whipped low across the penalty area, passing through a forest of tired limbs. It seemed as if it was going to escape out the other side, untouched, until somebody managed to slide in at the far post and hook a foot round it. Ball and the birthday boy finished up in the net together.

Martin's laughing teammates hauled him to his feet and began to jog back towards the centre-circle. 'Four goals!' cried Ross, the captain. 'Magic!'

'Just one of them days,' grinned Martin, affecting a false modesty.

'Sure is. I wish it was your birthday every time we played.'

The referee decided enough was enough and blew for full-time before Fyleden could kick off yet again. While the stripe-shirted players danced off the pitch singing 'Happy Birthday!', the visitors trailed across to receive some words of consolation from their teacher.

'Hard luck, lads, you did your best,' said Mr Tyler with a shrug. 'Nobody can ask for more than that. There's no disgrace in losing when the other team plays like they did today. Everything went their way.'

'I just hope we're at full strength by the time we meet them in the league,' said Stuart. 'Oz should be back in goal by then.'

'I think we need him fit again sooner than that – and the others who were missing today,' replied Mr Tyler. 'Our next Cup match is straight after half-term against the Saints.'

Result:	Oakfield	5 v 1	Fyleden
	h-t:	3 – 0	
Scorers:	Hudson	(4)	McCann
	Ward		

. . . too early yet to publish a group table, but someone else is soon appearing in print – let's have a read of the first Captain's Log *entry in a copy of* Up the Saints!, *the monthly magazine written by the pupils of St Wystan's . . .*

UP THE SAINTS!
Captain's Log – Saturday 4 October

Not exactly a brilliant start to our County Cup campaign. We lost 2-1 at home to the holders, Shelthorpe, today. Pity! Our other two games are both away so it's going to be a tough task to qualify now.

Our Man of the Match must have been Jagdish Hira on the right wing. Jag scored a great goal and we might have had one or two more before half-time with a bit of luck. After that, there was really only one team in it – and it wasn't us.

Anyway, the Saints go marching on to play Fyleden after half-term. People reckon they're the weakest team in the group – so let's hope that's right.

Our league form's been good so far – played 2, won 2, with David Butler top scorer with 5 goals – so maybe we still have an outside chance in the Cup if Shelthorpe slip up.

All credit to them for the way they fought back this morning but we were dead disappointed to lose. Mr Cooper was well narked, too, the way we conceded two goals close together, even though he tried not to show it as referee. Our full-back, Ben Udal, said he heard him swear when they scored their winner!

All for now – signing off till next time.

Simon James, 7C

HALF-TERM

. . . scene: Fyleden recreation ground on Friday afternoon – looks like some of the footballers are putting in a bit of extra practice during the holiday . . .

'C'mon, Bandit, try and get your crosses higher,' called out Stuart Kaye, the school team captain, in frustration. 'You can't expect Neil to get his head to them down there.'

'Well, he can kick the ball instead.'

'Yeah, and so can other people. What's the use of having a giraffe in the team if you're going to aim at his knees?'

Stuart had arranged this special get-together in order to see how many of his squad were likely to be available for their game against St Wystan's. He broke off from watching the heading practice to check on their first-choice goalkeeper. 'How's the wrist feel, Oz?' he asked.

Oz was gingerly catching a ball thrown to him by Graham, his reluctant stand-in. It was the first time Oz had handled a ball since damaging himself in a playground fall only a couple of

29

weeks into the term. He pulled a face. 'Still jars a bit,' he admitted, 'but don't tell Tyler that or he won't pick me next week.'

'It's no good playing if you're not fully fit. You'll only make it worse.'

'I know, I know, but there's still a few days left yet. I should be OK by Wednesday.'

Stuart wasn't so sure. He'd rather have Graham in goal again than risk Oz letting shots in because of his injury. 'Well, don't overdo it here, just take it easy. You don't have to prove to us how macho you are.'

They grinned at each other. 'Sure, another few minutes of this then I'll take some shots at Graham,' said the goalkeeper. 'Just in case he does have to play again.'

The captain left them to it and took over the job of trying to mark Neil as the crosses came in from either flank. The only way to beat the long-legged Neil in the air was to judge the flight of the ball better and time the jump well to meet it first. It was no easy task, as Stuart had found to his cost at primary level. Neil had scored twice in both matches between their schools last season, a fact that the striker had not been slow to remind him about when they met up again at the Community College.

There were three attackers and two defenders to challenge for the centres, but Stuart laid down the rule that goals could only be scored with headers. The quality of the crosses was still rather mixed, often too low or wide of the intended targets, but gradually the wingers found their range – and Neil's head – more regularly.

'Goal!' cried Neil as the ball glanced off the post and went in. 'Unstoppable. No keeper would've got near it.'

'Yeah, I'll give you that one,' Stuart conceded. 'Best effort yet. Let's have a few more like that from you.'

The captain didn't mind how many goals Neil scored in practice as long as they helped to play him into form and boost his confidence enough to repeat the performance in a match situation. They'd lost both their league games so far, as well as the Cup-tie.

The next centre was also met with a firm forehead, but this one belonged to midfielder Ronnie. He had darted forward to make contact at the near post and powered a bullet header into the goal. As there was no net to trap the ball, his reward was to go and fetch it from the hedge behind.

'Great stuff, Ronnie!' Stuart called out. 'We've missed you the last two games. Are you OK again now?'

Ronnie smacked the ball back out to Bandit for another go. 'Sure, fine. Can't wait to get back into action. Got fed up lying in bed all day while you lot were enjoying yourselves at school.'

'I bet you did,' Neil chuckled. 'It's time for you to do your share of the work now. If defences see you're good in the air too, they won't all be marking me. They'll have somebody else to worry about.'

It was soon Stuart's turn to demonstrate his own heading ability. He took off from his right leg with a huge spring, arched his back and then his neck muscles snapped his head forward like a mousetrap, clearing the ball away well outside the area.

'Wow! Wicked header, skipper!' cried Bandit. 'You almost scored in the other goal.'

Stuart laughed. 'Just making sure these attackers don't get their own way all the time. Can't have them getting too big-headed.'

'Thought that's exactly what you did want, skipper,' joked Ronnie. 'The bigger the head we've got, the better!'

. . . no need to be afraid to head the ball – it won't hurt as long as you know how to do it properly. Check things out with the County Coach . . .

HEADING

You don't have to be tall to be a good header of a ball, although a bit of extra height might help you beat somebody else to it. There's more to successful heading than meets the eye – or preferably the forehead!

Want to improve your own heading skills? Take a few tips from me.

✓ Watch the ball all the way – keep your eyes OPEN

✓ Always make contact with the forehead to avoid injury

✓ Use your body and firm neck muscles to gain extra power

✓ You strike the ball – don't wait for it to hit you

✓ Time jump to meet ball at highest point of your flight

✓ Attacking – head top half of ball to direct it downwards at goal

✓ Defending – head bottom half of ball to gain height and distance

✓ Passing – glance or guide ball to teammate to keep possession

✓ Keep practising – with friends or against a wall

GREAT HEADER!

FYLEDEN v ST WYSTAN'S

Wednesday 22 October
k.o. 3.45 p.m.
Referee: Mr K. Tyler

... time for one last game before the clocks change and it becomes too dark to play after school – the Saints left Brinkwood early to journey across the South Quarter to Fyleden, with both teams hoping for their first Cup victory ...

Oz kicked the foot of the post, a habit of his before the start of a match to knock any mud off his boots. The goalkeeper did it this time more out of irritation. He wasn't even wearing his football boots.

'Pack that up, will you, Oz,' said Graham. 'You're putting me off.'

Oz scowled. 'I should've been playing today, I'm fit enough. Serves Tyler right if we go and lose again now.'

'Thanks for the vote of confidence,' Graham muttered. 'Look, I'm sorry, Oz, but I don't want you standing there, breathing down my neck and ready to criticize when I make a mistake.'

'Don't you mean *if* you make a mistake?'

'No – *when*,' Graham sighed.

They didn't have to wait long for that to happen. Five minutes into the game, the Saints centre-forward David Butler slipped the ball between two defenders and his captain found another gap to exploit – the one Graham had left between himself and the near post, something goalies should never do.

'That's one to put in your log,' laughed David as they trotted back to the halfway line. *'The captain picked his spot and coolly steered the ball home.* Only make sure you give me a namecheck as well for the assist.'

Simon smiled. 'I'll only give you a mention if you score as well.'

'Consider it done.'

Graham glanced guiltily over towards Oz who was now lurking near the corner flag. He hardly needed to guess what Oz would be thinking.

By contrast, Mark Brown at the other end was leaning against one of his goalposts, the very picture of contentment. He'd only had to deal with a back-pass so far, but he was soon to be shaken rudely out of his slumbers.

The keeper was slow to appreciate the danger when Fyleden attacked up the right wing, thinking that his defenders had everyone well covered. As the ball was crossed, Mark started to go for it then decided to leave it to his centre-back, Steve Varley, to deal with instead. Steve saw his keeper make an initial move, hesitated, and both of them were caught in no man's land. A yellow shirt soared past Steve and there was a thud as the ball struck the boy's forehead – and there was another even more solid thud as it clattered against the crossbar and rebounded away.

'Unlucky, Neil,' yelled Bandit. 'Great header.'

There was a louder shout from the Saints teacher Mr Cooper on the touchline. 'Let's have some calling, Greens. Sort it out. You can't give that big kid free headers like that.'

It was a lucky escape for the Saints and they learnt from it. Any feelings of complacency quickly disappeared. They all remembered how they had let slip a slender 1–0 lead against Shelthorpe – and lost the match. Their talented midfield trio worked hard to gain control of that battleground, strangling most of Fyleden's attacks at birth and using it as a launch pad for Saints assaults into enemy territory.

The second goal came shortly before half-time. Steve went up for a corner and gave Fyleden a taste of their own medicine. Neil failed to drop back and mark him and the defender rose to meet the captain's in-swinging corner with a firm, well-placed header beyond Graham's reach.

The home team huffed and puffed throughout the second period to little effect, rarely causing any alarms in the visitors' goalmouth. The service to Neil dried up and he had no further chance to practise his heading. They had Stuart Kaye, their captain, to thank for the fact that the Saints only added one more goal. Stuart led a well-organized, rearguard action to keep the score down, but he couldn't prevent David getting his name into the magazine again, as promised. The striker finished off a five-man passing move with a delicate chip over the stranded keeper into the net.

As the disconsolate Fyleden players trudged into school, their Cup ambitions already in ruins, the Saints gathered excitedly around their teacher.

'A fine all-round team performance, well played,' said Mr Cooper in praise. 'We're still in with a shout now, especially if Shelthorpe and Oakfield draw on Saturday. That'd be the best result for us.'

'What if one of them win?' asked Simon.

The teacher rubbed his chin ruefully. 'Then we're in a spot of trouble, I'm afraid, lads – but I'll try not to let any of you hear me swear this time!'

Result:	**Fyleden**	**0 v 3**	**St Wystan's**
		h-t: 0 – 2	
Scorers:			**James, Varley**
			Butler

VANDALS

. . . the Fyleden players were not the only ones whose half-term efforts lay in ruins – vandals had been at work too at Shelthorpe . . .

'What a mess!' exclaimed Matt, the team captain, in horror.

The footballers had turned out for their usual Monday practice session, despite the disruptions to the rest of their daily routine in school caused by the vandalism. They hadn't minded the cancelled lessons where ransacked classrooms were still unfit for use, and had even put up with long queues for the remaining undamaged toilets, but this was different. They took the wreckage of their goalposts very personally.

A terrible sight met their eyes as the boys stared over the playing fields at the soccer pitches. Broken, jagged pieces of crossbars littered the penalty areas while some of the wooden posts, snapped in half, leant crookedly in their sockets.

'Could be worse, I guess,' sighed Liam, pointing towards a pitch in the far corner. 'At least there's one set of goals still standing.'

'Yeah, but look at the size of them,' groaned Tom, the goalkeeper. 'They're not meant for kids our age. I won't even be able to touch the bar.'

'We're lucky to have any bars left at all,' replied his centre-back. 'It'll be the same problem for both sides.'

'Can't see it being a low-scoring match with Oakfield on Saturday, can you?' said Sadiq, hoping he might be able to add to his own goals tally more easily. 'Especially with Hudson playing. He's wicked.'

'Don't remind me,' Liam muttered. 'I'm the one who's gonna have to mark him.'

Several of them knew Martin Hudson from the South Quarter area team. They'd already heard about his four goals in the Cup before he went out and scored another hat-trick in South's first match against the North.

'He'll think it's his birthday again when he sees these massive goals,' Tom murmured as they reached the pitch and he gazed up at the crossbar high above his head.

'Sorry I'm late, lads,' said their teacher when he eventually arrived on the scene. 'Had a few things to sort out with the Head. Mr Smith isn't keen to spend more money on new posts, I'm afraid. It's the second time this has happened in two seasons.'

'Does anybody know who's to blame, Mr Calvert?' asked Matt.

The teacher shook his head. 'What makes me really sick is that it's probably ex-pupils. They certainly seemed to know where all the expensive things are kept, but fortunately they couldn't break the security locks. They just went around smashing the place up instead.'

Matt nodded. 'We saw the sports shed door had been ripped off.'

Mr Calvert pulled a face. 'Yes, they helped themselves to some of our P.E. equipment.

That's all got to be replaced now as well.'

The delayed session began with some work on ball control and passing skills. Then as the light started to fade, Mr Calvert organized an eight-a-side game between the penalty areas to prepare for their next Cup match. He was cheered up a little by the form his players showed. The highlight for him was a swift, one-touch passing move that Sadiq finished off with a fierce half-volley. The ball flew well out of Tom's reach in the coned goal.

Tom wasn't best pleased when the teacher gave a goal. 'That would've gone over the bar,' he complained.

'Quite right, Tom – normally,' said Mr Calvert, grimacing. 'But not in the big goals we'll have to use on Saturday.'

'That's not fair.'

'No, it isn't. But you try telling the vandals that.'

On his way home, Matt took a short cut through the park, even though he'd been told not to now that it was getting dark so early. The paths were illuminated at intervals and Matt felt safe enough as he jogged steadily along, thinking about what team Mr Calvert might pick to play Oakfield.

He was taken totally unawares by the ambush. All of a sudden, three youths jumped out of the bushes in front of him.

'Gotcha!'

It only took him a few moments to recover from his fright. 'You idiot!' he snapped. 'Thought I was gonna be mugged or something.'

'See the way he speaks to his big brother,' cackled one of the youths. 'No respect, kids, these days.'

'Leave off, Jaz,' Matt said. 'I want to get back for tea. I'm hungry.'

'Bet we scared the pants off yer then.'

'No way. I knew it was you,' he retorted. 'What are you lot doing, anyway, hanging around here in the dark?'

'Just been havin' a game of footie. Nowt else to do, is there, when you're unemployed.'

Matt noticed a football under the arm of one of his brother's mates and peered at it more closely. 'Hey, that's one of ours!' he exclaimed. 'Calvert always marks the sports stuff like that with a big letter S.'

'So? What's that got to do wiv us?' snarled the ball-carrier.

'We've had some gear nicked, that's what. The whole school's been done over.'

The youth gave a smirk. 'Nuffink to do wiv us, is it, Jaz – you tell 'im.'

'Yeah, that's right, we just found this ball in the park,' said his brother, wrapping an arm round Matt's shoulder. 'C'mon, our kid, I'll make sure yer get home safely. See yer later, guys.'

Matt was led away under protest. 'He's got our ball. I want it back.'

'Just shut it, will yer,' Jason warned him when they were on their own. 'It's none of your business.'

'Yes it is. It's my school that's suffered – and my team,' he moaned, realizing that Jason himself must have been one of the vandals. 'We're gonna have to play in big goals now 'cos of your gang.'

'Who cares?'

'I do – I might've guessed you'd be involved.'

'What d'yer mean by that?'

'Well, you're not exactly unknown to the police, are you? They've been round our house a couple of times in the past 'cos of things you've got up to. You're gonna get yourself locked up one of these days.'

'What yer gonna do – grass on your own big brother to the cops?'

'No, course not,' Matt sighed, helpless. He felt like hitting Jason, he was so mad at him.

'Found out summat you don't know, anyway,' Jason cackled.

'Oh yeah, and what's that? How long it takes to smash goalposts?'

'No, saw summat on Smithy's desk when we trashed his office – a letter of resignation.'

Matt was mildly interested, despite himself. 'Is the Head leaving?'

Jason sniggered, knowing how much his next statement was going to upset his soccer-mad brother even more. 'No, Calvert is!'

'I don't believe you. You're just making that up.'

'Straight up, I tell yer. Old Calvert's handed his notice in. Your precious team's losin' its coach at Christmas!'

Matt was still feeling stunned next morning as he read the teamsheet Mr Calvert had put on the sports noticeboard. He wondered how he could let his teammates into the secret without giving his brother away.

He sighed. 'Perhaps it's better if they don't know anything yet – at least not before the Cup match.'

COUNTY CUP – home v. Oakfield
Sat 25th Oct K.O. 10 o'clock
Be at school by half past 9

Team: 4 – 2 – 4
T. Humphreys
J. Butcher R. Cheetham L. Walsh S. Hinton
M. Eales (Capt) J. Naylor
K. Ashby I. Strong S. Jilani J. Shaw

Subs: H. Gladwin, C. Rai, A. Morgan.

SHELTHORPE v OAKFIELD

Saturday 25 October
k.o. 10 a.m.
Referee: Mr R. Calvert

. . . there are always plenty of goals to see when Oakfield are playing – especially if the goals themselves are bigger than usual . . .

It didn't take Martin Hudson long to make his mark on the game. He deliberately lofted his first shot well over the keeper's head and watched the ball drop underneath the high crossbar into the net.

So did the keeper. There was nothing Tom could have done to stop the ball going in. He stared at the referee and spread his arms in a theatrical gesture of helplessness.

What am I supposed to do about that? was his unspoken message.

Mr Calvert's response was also in mime. He pointed back up the field towards the centre-circle to signal the goal and gave Tom a little shake of the head in sympathy.

Matt wasn't quite so silent, cursing his brother under his breath. 'If we lose this game because of him and his mates, I'll shop the lot of them.'

By half-time, however, the captain was in a much happier frame of mind. The Cup holders had turned the vandalism to their own advantage, using the extra space on the larger pitch well, and were now leading 3–1. Whenever Oakfield's attacks broke down, their over-ambitious wing-backs tended to be caught out of position too far upfield and Shelthorpe's wingers fully exploited the holes in the visitors' threadbare defence.

Revelling in their unexpected freedom, Kevin Ashby and Jonathan Shaw helped themselves to a goal each, and Kevin provided the cross for Sadiq to slide home the third just before the interval.

'Well done, lads, keep this up,' Mr Calvert praised them. 'A victory today will put us in the clear at the top of the table.'

'Yeah, and we've only got Fyleden to play after this – and they're useless,' grinned Kevin. 'We'll be in the semis then.'

Matt glanced at the teacher's face, but Mr Calvert was giving nothing away. Nobody else knew that he wouldn't be around after Christmas to help them defend the trophy that Shelthorpe won last season.

'C'mon, team, big effort,' urged the captain. 'Don't let them get back into this game. They'll be pumped up for the second half now, you bet.'

Matt was right. Oakfield swarmed forward in an almost reckless policy of all-out attack, throwing caution to the winds in their desperation to score more goals. Driven on by captain Ross Collins, they took huge risks, often leaving their own goal terribly exposed to counter-attack – but after ten minutes of non-stop bombardment, the gamble paid off. Ross swept the ball out wide to one of his wing-backs whose charge was ended when he cut inside and fell victim to Matt's late, lunging tackle.

'Direct free-kick,' announced Mr Calvert. 'Steady, Matt.'

Shelthorpe's ramshackle wall of bodies was not built to withstand a blast from Martin Hudson. Basic instincts of self-preservation took over as Martin's lethal rocket flew straight at them. The wall crumbled and parted in disarray, giving the keeper little time to react as the ball burst through a gap.

Tom's save was magnificent. He hurled himself full-length to his right and got a firm hand on the ball to turn it against the post.

He was unlucky. The ball bounced back into play and Martin's strike-partner, Sunjit Gill, had the simplest of tap-ins, unchallenged.

'Where was the marking?' Matt stormed at his teammates. 'You were like a load of statues, just standing around doing nothing. C'mon, get a grip. We want to be in the semis, even if Calvert doesn't.'

They looked at him in puzzlement, not understanding his meaning, and Matt made no attempt to explain. Nor was there any time to do so. The Shelthorpe players were all far too busy trying to cling on to their fragile lead as Oakfield kept them under constant pressure. Goals change games, and if Oakfield had managed to equalize, they might well have gone on to win the match.

As it was, the next goal was scored at the other end. A hefty clearance from Liam sailed over the halfway line and also over the heads of the Oakfield centre-backs. Ian Strong won the sprint race for the ball. The Shelthorpe number eight outpaced both defenders, pushed the ball past the advancing keeper and then steered it into the empty net from a narrow angle.

The breakaway fourth goal killed Oakfield's fightback dead in its tracks. Even Martin let his head go down. He knew there would be no hat-trick glory for him today now.

Result:	Shelthorpe	4 v 2	Oakfield
		h-t: 3 – 1	
Scorers:	Ashby, Shaw		Hudson, Gill
	Jilani, Strong		

. . . *let's see how the group table is shaping up after two matches . . .*

CUP STATS

GROUP TABLE

	P	W	D	L	Goals F	A	(GD)	Pts
Shelthorpe	2	2	0	0	6	3	(+3)	6
Oakfield	2	1	0	1	7	5	(+2)	3
St Wystan's	2	1	0	1	4	2	(+2)	3
Fyleden	2	0	0	2	1	8	(−7)	0

Analysis

Cup holders Shelthorpe look well placed to reach the semi-finals of the competition again. Three points clear at the top, their final game is at home to bottom team Fyleden, who are sadly now out of contention. Only the group winners will qualify for the knockout stage of the County Cup. Before that match, Oakfield play host to St Wystan's with each school having the chance to leapfrog over Shelthorpe, temporarily at least, on goal difference (GD)*. At present, Oakfield are above the Saints by dint of having scored more goals.

Leading Cup scorers

5 – Hudson (Oakfield)
2 – Jilani (Shelthorpe)

* Note: *3 points for a win, 1 point for a draw*
Goal difference worked out by subtracting goals against from goals for

UP THE SAINTS!

Captain's Log – Tuesday, 28th October

A good victory to report this time in the County Cup. The Saints won 3-0 away at Fyleden last week. Even yours truly managed to get his name on the scoresheet for only the second time this season.

Leading scorer David Butler added another goal to his total (promised you'd get a mention, Dave!) and defender Steve Varley powered home a header. We were so much on top, our keeper Mark Brown could have taken this mag out to read during the match, although that's perhaps not a good idea – my diary might have sent him to sleep!

Trouble is, we've just heard today that the holders, Shelthorpe, also won again, beating Oakfield 4-2, so we haven't really got much hope now of qualifying for the semis. First we've got to beat Oakfield ourselves and then pray that Fyleden pull off a miracle by defeating Shelthorpe. No chance! Mr Cooper says football's a funny old game, but that'd be ridiculous.

So what's going to happen now? Who knows? Watch this space . . .

All for now – signing off till next time.

Simon James, 7C

RUMOUR

. . . it's November now and new sets of goalposts have arrived at Shelthorpe School in time for their double clash with Fyleden in both league and Cup . . .

Matt and his midfield partner Jack left the dining hall together and stood gazing at the trophy cabinet in the foyer. It was packed full of trophies of all shapes and sizes, ranging from a small wooden knight for the school chess champion to a bronze statuette of a rugby player awarded to Shelthorpe for winning the under-15 South Quarter Sevens tournament.

Pride of place, however, right in the centre of the cabinet, went to the brightly polished, silver County Cup that was captured last season by the previous Year 7 soccer squad.

'It's incredible how no school in the South managed to win the Cup for fifteen years,' said Jack. 'I gather it usually goes to one of the North or East outfits.'

The captain nodded, still in awe of the gleaming trophy with its ornate, curved handles, even though he hardly ever passed through the foyer without stopping to stare at it. 'Yeah, but

we're gonna make sure it stays right here now
we've got it,' Matt replied in a manner that
brooked no argument. 'The only time it leaves
this cabinet is to be presented to us again in the
spring.'

'Must weigh a ton. Are you sure you're going
to be able to lift it above your head without dropping it?'

'No trouble. It's something I keep dreaming
about.'

'You'll have to ask Calvert to let you have a practice with it before the Final.'

'Depends if he's still here,' said Matt, pulling a face.

'How d'yer mean? Course he'll still be here,' Jack scoffed, then his certainty began to fade as he looked at his captain. 'Won't he? Do you know something I don't?'

Matt gave a little shrug, as if trying to pass it off. 'Oh, just a rumour going round, that's all.'

'First I've heard of it. Where's he going?'

'Dunno. Like I said, it's only a rumour. But he might be leaving at Christmas, so it's reckoned.'

Matt had decided that might be the best way of getting the burden of the secret off his chest – start up a rumour himself and see what everybody's reaction was. While he let Jack brood upon the news for a few moments, Matt continued to peer into the glass showcase.

'Anyway, we've got to win this thing again first,' he said, pointing to the large Quarter Shield sitting next to the County Cup.

'Yeah, retaining the Shield would make a nice sort of farewell present for Calvert, I guess,' Jack sighed. 'If he *is* really leaving, that is. Wonder who might take over from him?'

'Doesn't matter who it is,' stated the captain

positively. 'We'll keep on winning, with or without Calvert.'

'Yeah, but he did coach last year's team, remember. He knows what it takes to win the Cup.'

'All it takes is goals,' Matt sneered. 'And now we've got some new ones, we'll christen them with a netful in the league on Saturday – and then stuff Fyleden again in the Cup in a fort-night.'

'Right!' Jack agreed. 'C'mon, time we went and got changed for the practice. Can't wait to tell the others about Calvert . . .'

Shelthorpe were in for a surprise. Fyleden put up much stiffer resistance in the league fixture than when the schools met in a pre-season friendly. Oz was back in action now and he made a string of outstanding saves to restrict the league leaders to three goals.

Matt himself had the honour of being the first to score in the new goals, driving the ball in off a post and leaving a muddy mark on the wood-work. Then Sadiq struck twice in the second half to record only a 3–0 victory.

'It'll be different in the Cup,' the captain insisted in the changing room afterwards. 'They just got lucky today. It could've been double figures if we'd taken more of our chances.'

'Yeah, I'd have had a hat-trick, if it weren't for that goalie,' said Ian Strong sourly. They all laughed and showered their boastful number eight with wet towels and smelly socks.

'Anybody can stop you scoring, Strongman, but he can't keep all our shots out,' Matt grinned. 'Nobody's gonna stand between us and that Quarter Shield.'

. . . the Cup holders seem confident enough – let's take a quick look behind the scenes now at Oakfield and St Wystan's to see how their squads are shaping up as they prepare to meet one another next week . . .

BE PREPARED

. . . at Oakfield, the players are having more shooting practice – as usual . . .

'Try and hit it first time if you can,' shouted Mr Bradley. 'Your go, Paul.'

The teacher passed the ball across the penalty area for Paul Ward to shoot at goal. The keeper dived, got a hand to the ball and pushed it round the post.

'Good save, Andrew, up you get quickly,' urged Mr Bradley.

Nathan was next in the firing line. His miskick fooled the keeper completely and the ball bobbled into the opposite corner of the goal.

'Lucky – next!'

Sunny netted easily, but captain Ross scooped his shot over the bar. Then up stepped Martin Hudson. He moved on to the ball smoothly and the others could hardly believe it when their leading scorer scuffed it wide of the target.

'Too casual, Martin,' Mr Bradley called after his embarrassed striker. 'Go and fetch it.'

It was Paul's turn again. He blasted this effort straight at Andrew who did well to stand his ground and hold on to the ball.

'Place it, Paul, no need to try and knock his teeth out. Next!'

The demanding teacher continued to feed balls to the group of players for another quarter of an hour. Some he rolled towards them, some he sent bouncing across at awkward heights and others he chipped over for headers, expecting the boys to take up the right position for an early strike at goal. Finally, he allowed them all a short breather – including the overworked keeper – in order to make a few coaching points.

'It's often worth shooting as soon as you can,' he began. 'You don't have to wait till you see the whites of the goalie's eyes. You might well catch him by surprise out of position. And if you delay too long, a defender can get in a tackle or block the shot.'

'I'm sometimes scared of messing up and wasting the chance,' Nathan admitted.

'Everybody misses – even Martin,' replied Mr Bradley, glancing at him pointedly. 'I won't complain if you miss, but I will if a shooting chance is there and you don't have a go. Remember the old saying in football . . .'

'If you don't shoot, you don't score!' they chorused and laughed. They'd heard the teacher say it dozens of times in the past two months.

'Right, well, don't you ever forget it,' he grinned. 'Goals win matches.'

Andrew White, Oakfield's regular keeper, decided it was best not to say anything. He didn't think Mr Bradley would care to hear his opinions about the team's usual tactics of all-out attack. The shooting practice had been too much like situations Andrew often faced in games – no defenders anywhere to be seen to help him out.

'Goals can *lose* matches too,' he muttered under his breath. 'And we give away far too many for my liking.'

. . . meanwhile, over at Brinkwood, the Saints are concentrating their efforts on defence . . .

Mr Cooper had decided to opt for a man-to-man marking system on Oakfield's twin spearhead of Martin and Sunny.

The teacher took his two best defenders to one side during the squad's lunchtime training session and explained what he had in mind.

'Martin's your man, Steve. We all know how good he is, but we've got to try and keep him quiet somehow. And I believe you're the one to do it.'

Steve Varley nodded, keeping his own reservations to himself. Privately, he didn't think he was quite up to the job. He'd seen Martin in action for the area team.

'And Sunny's your responsibility, Ben. Keep tight on him wherever he goes. Make him think he's got an extra shadow.'

'What if they give us the slip?' Ben Udal asked.

'It's up to you to make sure that they don't,' said Mr Cooper. 'But if it does happen, the nearest teammate will just have to try and cover for you.'

The two boys wandered away to join in the practice game again. 'Phew!' breathed Steve.

'Sounds like we've both got our work cut out on Saturday. Give either Martin or Sunny too much room and we're dead. Those guys just don't miss.'

'Just have to hope they have an off day,' Ben grinned. 'Don't envy you, having to look after Martin. I reckon you drew the short straw there.'

Steve sighed. 'Well, at least I stopped that Neil scoring when we played Fyleden. Perhaps I can do it again with a bit of luck.'

'I'd make that a *lot* of luck, if I were you,' said Ben to tease him. 'You never know, Martin might even be away or something.'

'Huh! In my dreams! I'm not *that* lucky.'

The team captain, Simon, came up to them. 'What did Coop have to say?'

Ben glanced at Steve before replying. 'Um, well, good and bad news really for you, I guess.'

'How d'yer mean?'

'Well, the good news is that you'll have plenty to write about in your next *Captain's Log* piece . . .'

'Oh yeah,' Simon replied slowly, suspecting that Ben was building up to a joke. 'And what's the bad news, then?'

'. . . I'm afraid he wants *you* to do a man-marking job on Martin Hudson!'

DEFENDING

A successful football team needs players who are good in defence. You don't want to concede more goals than you score!

Want to improve your own defending skills? Take a few tips from me.

- ✓ Marking: try and keep goal-side of opponent – nearer the goal than him
- ✓ Man-to-man marking – stay close to opponent and follow him
- ✓ Zonal marking: cover a certain area and mark anyone who comes into it
- ✓ Close down opponent – deny him time and space to play
- ✓ Tackling: block middle of ball with inside of boot – brace foot
- ✓ Tackling: bend knee for balance and strength – get full weight behind ball
- ✓ Try and stay on your feet when tackling – don't dive in
- ✓ Safety first – don't clear ball across your own goal
- ✓ Stay cool – don't panic!
- ✓ Keep practising your skills

MARK UP!

OAKFIELD v ST WYSTAN'S

Saturday 15 November
k.o. 10 a.m.
Referee: Mr M.Bradley

...let's follow the action from the soundtrack of a camcorder's built-in microphone – Mr James is recording the game's highlights and trying to do a running commentary to help Simon with his next diary entry...

'Oh dear, only a couple of minutes gone and there's the first goal. Oakfield's number ten, the scorer – I think he's the one called Sunny. The marking went to pot. I don't know where Ben was, but the ball's in the back of our net . . .

'. . . The Saints' defence seems all-at-sea with this man-to-man marking business – we could have been two down now if that Martin Hudson had just been a bit sharper in front of goal. I thought he was supposed to be good . . .'

Mr Cooper's voice picked up on the tape . . .
C'mon defence, mark up! Steve, Ben – get
tight on your men – don't let them turn with
the ball.

' . . . At last, a decent move by the Saints –
Simon's cross was put just over the bar by David
– good effort . . . that's more like it . . .

'. . . Hudson doesn't seem quite with it to me –
Steve's got him well shackled now – he's so close,
he's almost inside his shirt . . .'

Ye-es! Great goal, Jag – the equalizer! We
deserved that – brilliant shot, eh?

'. . . I bet you heard that – Mr Cooper's just
come running past me, a big grin on his face.
Fine goal by Jag – stuck the ball right in the
corner . . .

' . . . Hudson's just missed a great chance to put
his team ahead again. He was too slow shooting
and Steve whipped the ball off his toes . . .

'. . . There goes the whistle for half-time – 1–1
the score – and can you see how white-faced
Hudson looks? I don't think the boy's well . . .'

Simon's voice is heard . . .
How's it going, Dad? Is it working OK?

'Sure, I think I managed to capture both the goals – keep this up, you're doing well after a dodgy start.'

 A draw's no good, though. We've got to win to catch Shelthorpe and – look, switch that thing off, please, will you, Dad. I can't just stand here talking to a camera . . .

'The second half is about to kick off, but not by Hudson. I saw him being sick at half-time and now he's been subbed. He clearly wasn't fit to play . . .

'. . . Here's Simon on the ball, taking on the full-back and beating him . . . he curls a cross into the area, but the goalie's come out a long way to make the catch – no, he's dropped it! There's an almighty scramble . . . a shot's blocked, then another – did that one go in? No? . . . Yes, it did, the ref's given a goal – the ball must have crossed the line – no idea who scored it . . .'

 Jag again, wasn't it? He's the one getting the congratulations – that's his second.

Good of old Maurice to give the goal against his own team – very sporting of him.

'. . . Well, well, the Saints are in the lead – another goal would clinch it, surely, but they won't score with shooting like that . . . Simon's just hoofed the ball over the bar from ten metres . . . he'll be disappointed with that effort . . .

'. . . Phew! Bit too close for comfort, that one – Oakfield nearly equalized. I thought our keeper had it covered, but the ball slithered past him and hit the post – could be the slice of luck we need . . .

'. . . Oh dear, I'm going to be in trouble now. I was just changing the tape when the Saints suddenly broke away and scored before I could get the new one in. Simon will go bananas when he finds out . . .'

 Good goal, that, by your Simon, eh, Mr James? He'll enjoy seeing that later on video.

'. . . Can't be long left now, only a few minutes – should be able to hold on to this 3–1 lead . . . wait, this looks dangerous, their captain's storming through the middle . . . he's going to shoot . . . he's scored! Great goal, have to give him that – looks like we're all in for a tense finish . . .

'. . . Dying seconds of the match and the Saints are really under the cosh . . . Oakfield are sending everybody upfield for this corner – hello, who's that with the yellow top? It's their goalie! Even he's come up to try and grab the equalizer. It's death or glory now . . . over comes the corner – oh, brilliant header! Steve outjumped the lot to head the ball clear and it's been whacked right up into the deserted Oakfield half. The chase is on – who's going to reach the ball first? Oh, the ref's blown up. What a spoilsport! I reckon we'd have scored a fourth goal there . . .'

 Magic game, eh, Dad – can't wait to watch it at home on the telly, especially my goal. I've never seen myself score before.

'Ah, yes, well, you're not going to believe this, Simon, but . . .'

CUP STATS

Latest match

Result: Oakfield   2 v 3   St Wystan's

h-t: 1 – 1

Scorers: Gill   Hira (2)

        Collins   James

GROUP TABLE

	P	W	D	L	Goals F	A	(GD)	Pts
St Wystan's	3	2	0	1	7	4	(+3)	6
Shelthorpe	2	2	0	0	6	3	(+3)	6
Oakfield	3	1	0	2	9	8	(+1)	3
Fyleden	2	0	0	2	1	8	(–7)	0

Analysis

With that exciting victory over Oakfield, St Wystan's have now gone top of the table. They are level with Shelthorpe on points and also goal difference, but are placed above them as they

71

have scored one more goal, seven to six. It could scarcely be closer, but the holders still have a game to play – at home to bottom team Fyleden. The Saints can only wait . . . and pray!

Leading Cup Scorers

5 – Hudson (Oakfield)
3 – Hira (St Wystan's)
2 – James (St Wystan's); Jilani (Shelthorpe); Gill (Oakfield)

LAST STRAW

. . . the footballers of Shelthorpe School have a terrible shock when they return to school after the weekend – the vandals have struck again, and this time with even more devastating results . . .

'I just can't believe it!' cried Liam, appalled at the trail of wreckage across the soccer pitches. All the goalposts had been vandalized. Not a single one was left unbroken.

'Who *are* these people?' demanded Jack angrily. 'Somebody must know who's doing all this damage.'

Matt bit his lip and looked away. He had a pretty good idea who it was. He felt betrayed – and sick to the pit of his stomach. It was almost as if he was somehow to blame himself and that he'd let his teammates down.

Gladys came running towards them, shouting. 'They've nicked it!'

'What you talking about?' Sadiq called out.

Gladys pulled up short, breathless. 'The County Cup! It's gone!' he gasped. 'And the Quarter Shield – the cabinet's been smashed.'

'What about all the other things in it?'

'I think they just took them two. I saw the caretaker sweeping up all the glass and there's this big space on the middle shelf where they were.'

Matt slumped to the ground, head in his hands. He didn't seem to care that the grass was wet. 'What are we gonna do now?' he wailed. 'We're playing Fyleden here on Saturday and we haven't got any posts.'

'Nor the Shield,' Liam muttered. 'You won't even be able to hold that up either.'

The boys were genuinely stunned by the loss of the soccer trophies. They knew that the posts would be replaced – eventually – but the trophies were a different matter altogether.

'What are people going to say when they find out the County Cup's been pinched?' groaned Jack. 'It's been around for yonks.'

'Get up, Matt,' said Sadiq, lending the captain a hand. 'Calvert's heading this way. He looks dead mad.'

'What's going to happen now, Mr Calvert?' asked Liam as the teacher came up to them. 'Will Saturday's game have to be cancelled?'

'No, we're not going to let these yobbos stop us playing,' said Mr Calvert. 'That's what I've come to tell you about. We need to fix up some transport now so ask your parents. I've switched the game to Fyleden.'

'You mean we've got to play the match away?' said Sadiq in dismay. 'Can't we just play somewhere else in Shelthorpe, like at our old primary school?'

The teacher shook his head. 'It's in the competition rules. If one team can't stage the fixture, no matter what the reason, they forfeit home advantage to the other school.'

'Doesn't matter,' said Liam defiantly. 'We'll still beat them at their place – we know we're much better than that lot, wherever we play.'

Mr Calvert looked at Matt, who was unusually quiet, but he guessed that the captain would be taking all this very hard. 'You've heard about the trophies, have you? I wish I could get my hands on those responsible. They must have a grudge against football – or me personally, maybe, I don't know.'

'Has anything else been stolen, Mr Calvert?' asked Jack.

He nodded. 'They obviously came back to finish off what they started at half-term. They've got away this time with tape recorders and televisions, plus several computers and other stuff. It's the last straw as far as I'm concerned.'

'How do you mean, Mr Calvert?' asked Matt, speaking for the first time and wondering whether the teacher would confirm that he was leaving.

'Well, I was going to tell you all sometime, so it might as well be now,' he sighed. 'You've probably heard the rumours, anyway. I'll be leaving Shelthorpe at Christmas – got a new job as deputy head elsewhere.'

'Who's going to be coaching us next term?' asked Liam.

'It's not decided yet. Somebody else on the staff may take over or perhaps the teacher who replaces me,' he replied, and then forced a wry grin. 'I've probably been here too long already. Everyone will be glad to see the back of me, I bet.'

'You won the County Cup last season,' said Jack simply.

'Yes, and now I've gone and lost it – so it'll be up to you people to make sure you win it again without me. At least that'll give the school more time to try and get the Cup back somehow.'

Matt was determined to do exactly that – and he knew just where to start his investigations . . .

. . . *wonder what* you *would do now in Matt's shoes? And more to the point, what steps do you think* he's *going to take to recover the Cup? Let's see . . .*

CONFRONTATION

. . . Matt storms into his brother's bedroom as soon as he arrives home from school . . .

'Oi, I've told yer before, our kid,' Jason snarled, hurriedly trying to stuff things into his wardrobe out of sight. 'Don't come bargin' into my room without knockin'. I need my privacy.'

'What you got in there you don't want me to see?' Matt demanded, ignoring the complaint. He was in no mood to let Jason act the big tough brother with him, despite the five years' difference in age.

'None of yer business.'

'Yes, it is. You know why I'm here. We've seen what you and your gang have done to the school again.'

Jason made a weak attempt at feigning innocence, but he couldn't keep a smirk off his face. 'Don't know what yer mean. What's happened at the school, then? Hope it's burnt down or summat.'

Matt made a bid to get to the wardrobe, but

Jason stepped in front of him to bar his path. 'Is the Cup stashed away in there?' he yelled.

'Course it ain't – don't be stupid. What would I want with that thing?'

'Well, where is it, then?' He was almost crying in frustration now as he struggled to get past, but Jason was strong enough to manhandle him away and flung him onto the bed.

'Cool it, kid. I'll beat yer to a pulp.'

Matt instantly bounced back up, fists clenched. 'I'd like to see you try,' he sneered. 'You can't knock me around any more like you used to.'

'Oh yeah, come on then, you want me to prove it?'

Matt was so angry, he might have called Jason's bluff if their mother hadn't banged on the door at that moment. 'What's going on in there?' she cried out. 'All that shouting. Calm down, the pair of you.'

The brothers stood glaring at each other across the room, breathing heavily. 'It's OK, Ma,' said Jason. 'Just Matt throwin' a little tantrum.'

Matt waited until it was clear that their mother wasn't listening at the door. 'If you don't tell me where those trophies are, Jaz, I'm going straight to the cops,' he said, slowly and deliberately, making quite sure his brother took him seriously. 'I mean it, no messing.'

'You wouldn't do that.'

'Yes, I would. You've gone too far this time, ruining our football and nicking the Cup and Shield. Tell me now or I'm gonna go and dial 999.'

'What, shop yer own brother?' Jason scoffed. 'Come off it.'

Matt nodded, white-faced, and started for the door. He'd never seen Jason move so fast. But as that route was blocked, Matt dashed to the wardrobe instead and flung it open. Cassette tapes, videos and a radio fell out onto the floor, all stamped with the name of Shelthorpe School.

'Where's the Cup, Jaz?' he repeated. 'If you want to end up in prison, that's up to you, but I'm asking you one last time – WHERE'S THE CUP?'

He was shouting again now and Jason clasped a hand over his brother's mouth. 'Belt up, will yer! You'll have Ma in here and I don't want her seein' all this stuff. She'll do her nut at me.'

Matt tore himself free. 'Good. And I hope she'll turn you in herself. So WHERE'S . . . ?'

'OK, OK, you win. I'll tell yer. We dumped 'em both in a ditch near the school. Knew somebody would find 'em there before too long. Just wanted to get a bit of revenge on old Calvert first.'

'Why, what's he done to you?'

'Plenty. He never liked me.'

'Surprise, surprise.'

'Just shut it and listen. Five years Calvert ran the soccer team in my year group and I never got a game. I hate his guts for that.'

'But you know how much the Cup means to me,' Matt sighed, slumping back onto the bed. 'And why did you have to go and smash up the posts as well? We've got to play the match away now 'cos of what you lot did.'

Jason gave a shrug. 'Yeah, well, soz about that. The others got a bit carried away, y'know.'

'No, I don't,' said Matt, standing up again. He was in control of the situation now. 'Show me where the trophies are later tonight when there's nobody about and then I'll pick them up in the morning on the way to school. I'll say it was just a hunch, thinking they might have been thrown away somewhere – and I got lucky.'

'Will Calvert believe that?'

'He might – coming from me. That's a risk you'll just have to take,' Matt said, before adding a warning. 'But if we go and lose out now on the title, I'll never forgive you. It'll be all your fault, Jaz – and I don't know what I might feel tempted to do then . . .'

FYLEDEN v SHELTHORPE

Saturday 22 November
k.o. 10 a.m.
Referee: Mr K. Tyler

. . . boosted by Matt's 'lucky' discovery of the trophies, Shelthorpe have brought the cleaned-up Quarter Shield with them, fully expecting to take it back home again after the match – but at half-time Fyleden are holding a shock 1–0 lead . . .

'No reason to panic, lads, there's plenty of time left yet,' Mr Calvert told his players. 'You were a goal down to the Saints and still went on to win, remember. And even a draw's good enough today to clinch the title.'

'We're bound to score soon,' Matt insisted. 'We must've had about ten shots to their one.'

'Yeah, but theirs went in,' muttered Liam, glancing accusingly at Tom, who had allowed the ball to slip through his hands into the net.

'Had the sun in my eyes,' scowled the goal-keeper as an excuse. 'I was nearly blinded.'

'Can't be helped, Tom – at least their keeper will have that problem in the second half,' the teacher pointed out.

Thirty metres away, the Fyleden party could scarcely believe their good fortune at being in front, but there was no luck involved with regard to Oz's goalkeeping. Shelthorpe had again found him in superb form.

'Make the most of this breather, Oz,' said Stuart Kaye, his captain. 'They're going to be coming hard at us again second half.'

'Suits me. The busier I am, the more I like it,' he grinned. 'Better than standing around, doing nothing and getting cold.'

'No danger of that this morning,' said Neil, their beanpole number nine. 'Even if we only end up drawing, that'll be a great result for us.'

'Not for the Saints, though,' put in Bandit, the goalscorer. 'A draw's no good for them – they need us to beat Shelthorpe.'

'Tough! I'm not bothered about what *they* need,' snorted Stuart. 'We're playing for our own pride here. We don't want to finish bottom of the group with no points.'

Although Matt might also have settled for a draw at half-time, he was still intent on winning the match to keep up Shelthorpe's one hundred per cent record in the group. 'C'mon, team, I've not found that Shield for nothing,' he cried as they lined up. 'I want to get my hands on it again in half an hour.'

At the other end, Oz was giving both of his posts a couple of sharp kicks as usual, as if to warn them what might happen if they let a goal go in. When he turned round, he found himself squinting into  the sun and pulled the peak of his cap down lower.

'Hope they don't start pinging in too many high crosses into the box,' he murmured. 'I'll hardly be able to see the ball coming.'

It was wishful thinking. As soon as the Shelthorpe right-winger, Kevin Ashby, received the ball, he tested the goalkeeper out with a speculative lob. Oz caught it all right, but the dazzling sun made his eyes water for the first time – though not the last. The frantic second period was played almost entirely in and around his penalty area, with Fyleden's forays into Shelthorpe territory becoming increasingly rare adventures.

Oz wasn't the only player having an inspired day. Stuart was also outstanding in central defence, organizing everyone around him to ensure they did their marking jobs properly. He virtually took on a sweeper's role, covering and tidying up after his teammates when they needed extra support. If a gap appeared, Stuart was there to plug it. If the ball ran loose, he was there to pick it up and clear.

And even when Shelthorpe did manage to evade Stuart's interceptions, they repeatedly came up against the green barrier called Oz. Three times he prevented what seemed certain goals, and then pulled off a double-save that was little short of miraculous. Having blocked Matt's volley on one side of his goal, he scrambled to his feet in time to spring up and tip a shot from Sadiq round the other post.

There were only about a dozen minutes to go when Shelthorpe eventually succeeded in finding a way past him. Kevin's cross from the right was cleverly flicked further on to the back post where Jack Naylor bundled the ball into the net off his knee. The equalizer would never have won any award for 'Goal of the Month', but its value to the holders was priceless.

Shelthorpe's celebrations might have gone on for some time if Matt hadn't cut them short. 'Save the party till after the match,' he ordered. 'It's not over yet. We need another goal to be safe.'

'C'mon, Matt, relax,' Kevin chided him. 'Tom's hardly had a touch this half. They're not even trying to score.'

'No, and we're not gonna give them the chance to either.'

Matt continued to drive his team forward, now in search of a winning goal, but Fyleden defended just as stubbornly. Ronnie headed an effort from Ian Strong off the line and Stuart thwarted his opposing captain with a well-judged, sliding tackle when Matt was poised to shoot inside the area.

They grinned at each other, both revelling in the tension of the match. 'Can't let you score again,' said Stuart.

Matt nodded, acknowledging the mutual

respect. 'Still time,' he replied.

Only just. Shortly afterwards, the referee checked his watch and saw the game had moved into the final minute. 'A draw's a fair result,' Mr Tyler murmured to himself as Bandit relieved the pressure by dribbling the ball over the halfway line. 'They've been far the stronger team, but we've defended like heroes. Nobody deserves to lose.'

Bandit had little intention of launching a serious raid, but when the full-back allowed him space to run on, he gratefully accepted the invitation. Instead of making towards the corner flag to use up more seconds, he left his casual marker for dead with a sudden burst of speed. Looking up, he saw Neil galloping through the middle, hoping for a cross, and Bandit duly obliged.

Only someone of Neil's height would have reached the lofted centre. The gangling striker soared into the air and glanced the ball off his forehead to deflect it goalwards, but despairing fingers clawed it out of the top corner.

They weren't Tom's. The hand belonged to the Shelthorpe captain.

'Penalty!' screamed the home supporters and players alike, and Mr Tyler could not ignore their appeals. He pointed to the spot and gave an apologetic shrug as if to say, 'What else can I do?'

Matt was saying more or less the same thing to his teammates. 'Had no choice,' he mumbled, almost in a state of shock. 'It would've gone in else.'

The referee had no heart to punish the boy further for deliberate handball. The penalty was enough. 'You take it, Ronnie,' he said simply.

Ronnie had already laid claim to the ball, keen to make amends for blazing Fyleden's only previous spot-kick this season over the crossbar. He had no pity on Shelthorpe.

'You've got to save it, Tom,' pleaded Matt, ashen-faced. 'If they score, we've had it.'

'Do my best,' grunted the goalie, tugging up his sleeves in a businesslike manner. Tom took some deep breaths to try and keep calm, hoping he looked more confident than he felt. His heart was racing.

'Last kick of the match,' announced Mr Tyler

as Ronnie placed the ball carefully on the muddy penalty spot. 'Time's up now so any rebounds won't count, OK? Understand, everybody?'

Even Oz came up to join the other players grouped around the edge of the area, but some of the Shelthorpe team had turned their backs. They didn't dare to watch. Their fate was now in Tom's hands – or Ronnie's right boot.

A deathly hush fell upon Fyleden's playing field. Matt was squatting on his haunches, staring at the goal as if in a trance. He became aware of the shrill blast of the referee's whistle, of Tom dancing about on his line to distract the kicker – and finally of the yellow, number eight shirt running in.

Ronnie 'The Rocket' Todd was a member of the hit-'em-hard school of penalty-taking, whose aim was to break the back of the net with the power of their shot. But he also wanted to make sure he didn't miss again.

'Keep it down,' he repeated to himself like a mantra as he approached the ball. 'Keep it down . . .'

WHACK!

. . . would you have the nerve to watch what happens? Does Ronnie score? Or does Tom save the penalty – and save his team from defeat? Turn over the page to find out – but only when you dare to look . . .

FINAL GROUP MATCH

Result: Fyleden 2 v 1 Shelthorpe
h-t: 1 – 0

Scorers: Crooke   Naylor
Todd (pen)

After Ronnie's fierce penalty kick smacked into the net – just where Tom had been standing before he dived to his left – there was no need for any presentation ceremony. The dejected Shelthorpe players trailed silently towards the school cloakroom to change, with only Matt pausing to gaze at the Shield for one last time.

'I know who's really to blame that we lost – and it's not me,' he muttered. 'I'm gonna get Jaz for this.'

Mr Calvert realized there was no consoling his captain at the moment. He waited until Matt went inside and then put the Shield back into his car boot. It wasn't being returned to Shelthorpe's repaired trophy cabinet, however. He was going to have to take it to its new home himself next week.

'Football can be a cruel game,' he mused, struck by the irony of the situation, 'but it's strange how things work out sometimes.'

He wouldn't be parted from the Shield for very long. They would soon be reunited when Mr Calvert became deputy headteacher at St Wystan's Comprehensive School, the new South Quarter Champions.

POSTSCRIPT

Captain's Log – Wednesday, 26th November

Amazing! The Saints are Quarter Champions! Who'd have thought it? Even the Year 7 footballers were gobsmacked when we heard that giantkillers Fyleden had slain the holders.

It's weird that Shelthorpe's teacher, Mr Calvert, is going to be our new deputy head. He came to morning assembly today to present the trophy to us. I was dead proud, holding the Shield up high on the stage, but a bit embarrassed too. He said we deserved to win it overall, but I'm not really sure that's true. Shows how much luck can play a part in the Cup, just like when we beat Oakfield 3-2 in our last group game.

The match was videoed and we all had a great laugh watching ourselves later, especially when their star striker was filmed being sick in the hedge! Jagdish Hira was the hero again with two more goals. Rumour has it that the third was scored by the captain, but the stupid cameraman - my dad - didn't record the goal. Typical!

Wonder if we're going to have joint managers next term with Mr Calvert here as well? That'd be good. Might even give us a better chance in the semis.

All for now - wishing the Saints a Happy New Year!

Simon James, 7C